The Jolly Old Woman Who Lived In A Shoe

Written by: Minnie McKnight
Illustrated by: Meri Dohmann

Fun For Kids Publishing

Canadian Cataloguing in Publication Data

McKnight, Minnie, 1917-1990
   The jolly old woman who lived in a shoe

ISBN 0-9685118-0-5

   I. Dohmann, Meri, 1953-   II. Title.

PS8575.K66J64 1999   jC813'.54   C99-900658-4
PZ7.M2174Jo 1999

A Fun For Kids Book

Published by Fun for Kids Publishing
Text © Ellen Kirk 1999

Illustrations © Ellen Kirk 1999

Published in Canada by
Fun For Kids Publishing
831 IOCO Road
Port Moody B.C. Canada
V3H 2W7
Phone: 1-604-469-3558
Fax: 1-604-469-3505
Printed and Bound in Canada

The Legacy

Everyone wants to give something special to their children. We received a legacy from our mother. It wasn't the usual sort of legacy of money or material things. It was found in an old leather bag on a yellowed piece of paper years after our mother had passed away and we thought we had lost it forever. It was a poem she wrote for us (her children) and she recited it as we sat around her. It gave us the emotional nourishment and stability that every child needs. It gave us the confidence that whatever happened we were needed and loved. We want to share this treasure with every parent and child in all stations of life.

Give your children a gift that will enrich their lives.

What do you do when you live in a shoe?
Everyone should know.

To Parents and Children
Everywhere

Artie

Ruthie

Junie

Kathy

Tillie

Bennett

Bun

Sue

Mary

Ellen

Jane

Willie

Shevi

Old Woman

Mitzy and Mattie

Billy and Ben were down on their knees,
They looked over the fence and through the trees.
There was a shoe like a house with a chimney up top,
The shoe had a door and a broom and a mop.

An Old Woman stood by with kids all around,
Laughing and playing with a happy loud sound,
This was strange; the boys were a little bit tense,
To live in a shoe just didn't make sense.

The Woman came by and stood at the gate,
They wanted to ask and just couldn't wait;
"What do you do when you live in a shoe?"
The woman just smiled as she looked at the boys,
To tell the story, was one of her joys.

This is what the Old Woman said:

There was an old woman who lived in a shoe,
She had so many children she didn't know what to do.
But they were so handsome and clever I'm told,
That she wouldn't trade one for diamonds or gold.

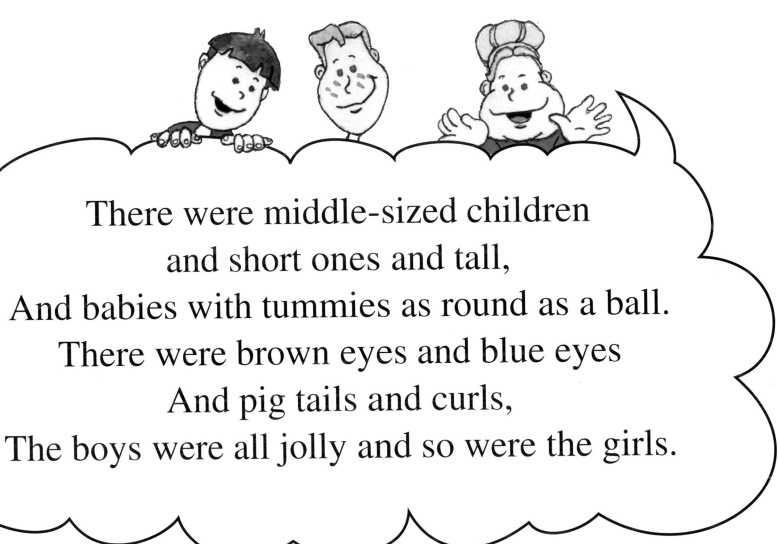

There were middle-sized children
and short ones and tall,
And babies with tummies as round as a ball.
There were brown eyes and blue eyes
And pig tails and curls,
The boys were all jolly and so were the girls.

They each had a bird or a dog or a cat
or a goat or a bunny or something like that.

The house that they lived in, both outside and in
Was clean as a whistle and neat as a pin.

Willie and Tillie and Bennett and Bun
Washed all the windows to let in the Sun.

Mary and Jane dusted the rooms
And swept the floors clean
with their own little brooms.

Ellen and Sue set the table at three
And put on the kettle for making the tea.

Ruthie made all of the cookies and bread,
And made each a big cake as high as their head.

Kathy knit sweaters and socks for the kittens,
And ironed their hankies and mended their mittens.

Artie made hats for the ponies and goats,
And fed them a sugar lump with their oats.

Junie climbed up on the roof it is said,
And painted the chimney a beautiful red.

She made each a pocketbook just the right size,
With a penny in each for a special surprise.

She made each a rain hat and slickers and boots,
And caps with a tassel and snow balling suits.

It's jolly as jolly to live in a shoe,
The children all shout and the Old Woman too.

Billy and Ben were smiling with glee,
They thanked the Old Woman for helping them see,
What you do when you live in a shoe.
Billy and Ben learned a lot that day,
They were happy inside as they went off to play.

When they got home they told Trudy and Sue,
We just learned the secret of life in a shoe.
It's not where you live, it's the things that you do,
We can all have life like the life in a shoe.
We can laugh and have fun and get everything done,
Look after our chores and play in the sun.

That night as they drifted to sleep in their bed,
They dreamt about what the Old Woman had said.